# Dirt Bike Adventure

## W. Wesley Miller

A **PERSPECTIVES** BOOK
**High Noon Books**
**Novato, California**

Series Editor: Penn Mullin
Cover Design: Damon Rarey
Illustrations: Herb Heidinger

International Standard Book Number: 0-87879-293-7

9   8   7   6
20  19  18  17  16  15  14

You'll enjoy all the High Noon Books. Write for
a free complete list of titles.

# Contents

# Chapter 1

# Friends

Dave stopped his Harley and took off his goggles. There was dirt all over his jacket. He looked at his watch. It was two o'clock. Joe and Willie would be here soon. Dave looked down at his bike. He had saved his money for over a year for this bike. It wasn't new but it was all his. His folks hadn't wanted him to buy a motorcycle, but he had wanted one so much. Finally they had agreed to let him have one. And he had proved he could be careful. He'd gotten only one ticket in ten months of riding. He had been going forty in a twenty-five mile zone. That had meant giving up the bike for a whole month. After Dave went to driver's school, the judge gave him back his license. No more speeding on the city streets, Dave decided. There were too many cops around the schools and drive-ins.

The roar of motorcycle engines made him look

up. Here came Joe and Willie. Joe was first to get there. He spun his bike around in a 180° curve as he stopped. Willie was right behind him. They were both yelling at each other.

"Ha! Beat you that time," yelled Joe.

"You were just lucky," shouted Willie. "If I hadn't spun out, you and that Yamaha would have lost."

"Oh, yeah?" said Joe. "Your bike couldn't beat a turtle!"

"Any time you're ready I'll take you on," shouted Willie. "Any time, any place."

"Hold it, hold it!" said Dave. "You two guys are always fighting. Don't you ever stop?"

"He thinks he's such a hot shot," said Joe loudly. "Ever since he got that Kawasaki all he wants to do is race."

"Yeah, and I can beat both of you," answered Willie. "Let the good times roll!"

"OK! OK, you two, do you want to fight or ride? Come on," said Dave, "let's climb some hills."

Joe and Willie slammed their bikes into gear. Then they sped up the hill behind Dave. After an hour they came to a stop. They had dirt and mud all over themselves.

"You know," Dave said, "we should really give

these bikes a workout."

"What kind of workout?" Joe asked.

"Yeah, what kind?" added Willie. "Do you want to race or something?"

"Race, race, race! Is that all you ever think of?" Joe yelled.

"No, I think about girls, too," answered Willie. "Bikes and girls."

"I sure hope you do better with the girls than you do with your bike," said Joe.

"Hey, man, what's wrong with my bike?" Willie yelled. He got off the Kawasaki and started towards Joe.

"Stop!" Dave shouted. "You guys want to prove who has the best bike? Let's really test them then."

"How?" asked Willie and Joe at the same time.

"Well," said Dave, "I thought we should try to cross Death Valley on our cycles. That would really prove who has the best bike."

Both boys were quiet for a short time. It was Joe who spoke first. "Death Valley? You must be crazy. It gets over 120 degrees out there in the day."

"Yeah, and colder than anything at night." added Willie.

"What's the matter?" asked Dave. "You guys

He got off his Kawasaki and started toward Joe.

afraid your bikes can't make it? Are you guys chicken?"

"I know my cycle could make it," said Joe.

'Hah," said Willie. "I bet you don't get halfway across!"

Willie turned to Dave. "When do we leave, buddy?"

"How about Tuesday?" asked Dave. "That will

give us two days to prepare."

"Fine with me," said Joe. "I'll tell my old man tonight."

"OK by me," said Willie. "My mom will fuss some but she'll let me go."

"Fine!" Dave said. "Then it is agreed that we'll go. Now we have to decide what to take with us."

"No problem!" Joe answered. "We each need a sleeping bag and some clothes."

"Don't forget some things to cook with," said Willie. "I sure want plenty to eat. I think we better take some tools with us, too."

"Right!" Dave replied. "And don't forget to bring a first-aid kit. We might need one."

"A map, don't forget a map!" Willie added. "I sure don't want to get lost out there in the desert. Man, that would be a real bummer!"

"Don't worry about a map," said Dave. "I'll take care of planning the route. I'll make sure we don't get lost."

"Hey!" Joe said. "We'd better bring canteens. It gets real hot out there. We'll need water with us all the time."

"Right," Dave agreed. "That's a good idea. OK, I think we've talked about everything. Just make sure you each bring your stuff. Pack your bikes so they are balanced. It makes it easier to ride."

"Oh, boy! I can hardly wait to get going," said Joe.

"Me, too!" Willie added.

"Good!" said Dave. "We'll all meet at Gil's gas station Tuesday morning at seven."

They all agreed on the time and the place to meet. Each rider would talk to his parents that night. They shoved their bikes into gear and started down the hill.

"Oh, boy, let the good times roll!" yelled Willie. They roared off through the dirt.

## Chapter 2

## The Trip

Dave arrived early at Gil's gas station. The morning was cool. He had his leathers zipped up to his neck. This kept the chill off when he rode. He would change his clothes when it got hot. He pulled off his helmet and looked at his watch. It was ten minutes to seven. Willie and Joe would be here soon.

Dave thought about his friends. They were all right guys even if they did fight all of the time. They had been friends for the last few years. They made good partners. Each of the three had special talents that helped the group. Sometimes Dave envied Joe and Willie. Joe lived with his dad and usually was on his own most of the time. His folks had been divorced for several years.

Willie's dad had been killed in an accident. He lived with his mother and kid sister.

The three friends spent time at each other's

houses. They all had little family problems. Boy, thought Dave, I wish I had only one parent to ask about going on this trip. Willie and Joe had to talk to only one parent each. On the other hand, Dave thought, having two parents can be nice, too. Whenever he had a problem, there was usually someone to talk to. His father had liked the idea of the Death Valley trip. His mom had been against it. But Dave's dad had talked her into letting Dave go. His dad had even called Willie's mom to try to help Willie go on the trip. Finally it was Dave's mom who helped plan the route. She also made up a shopping list for the boys.

It might be OK to have just one parent, Dave thought. But having two is all right, too.

Just then Willie drove up on his two-wheeler. It was two minutes to seven. "Where's the Yamaha Kid?" he yelled over the roar of his engine.

"He'll be here soon," answered Dave. "You got everything you need?"

"Sure do," said Willie. "Food, sleeping bag, first-aid kit, and a change of clothes."

"Good," said Dave. "I have the route all mapped out. We'll leave as soon as Joe shows up."

Both boys looked up as they heard the sound of Joe's bike. He hung a right off Fourth Street. Then he skidded to a stop in front of them.

"You guys ready?" asked Joe.

"Ready, willing, and able," answered Willie. "Let's go!"

Dave and Willie pulled on their helmets. Then they stepped on their foot shifts. The engines roared as they started to move. The three young riders pulled out and headed for the desert.

It was six o'clock when they stopped for the night. The first day had been fun but not too much happened. They had stopped for lunch and gas at a small drive-in near the desert. The cycles were in good running order. They had stopped again at three to gas up and check their map.

Each rider carried an extra gallon of gas strapped to his bike. According to the map, they might need extra gas at times. They all agreed that it was better to be safe then sorry.

All three riders were happy to stop for the night. Biking could be fun, but it was hard work, too. Their muscles ached after sitting all day on their cycles. It felt good to stretch out again. They cooked up a pot of franks and beans, boiled some coffee, and had dinner. After dinner they rolled out their sleeping bags and went to bed.

9

## Chapter 3

# Breakdown

"Hey! You guys going to sleep all day?" shouted Willie.

Dave and Joe opened their eyes. Willie was standing by a small fire with a cup in his hand. The sun was just coming up over the mountains.

"Oh, my aching back," groaned Dave. "I hurt all over."

"Me, too," said Joe, rubbing his eyes.

"Come on, you two," shouted Willie. "Coffee's hot and I brought some fruit to eat."

The three friends ate their breakfast and talked about the day's ride. Then they put out the fire and rolled up their sleeping bags. Each rider packed his bike and got ready to go. Then they took off across the desert. Dust, dirt, and rocks flew up behind them.

They had been on the trail for about three hours. Suddenly Joe's bike slid to a stop. Dave and Willie saw Joe stop. They turned and went back.

"Hey, what's wrong?" asked Willie.

"Oh, it's that darned chain," said Joe. "It just broke on me."

"No sweat," said Willie. "We'll have it fixed in no time."

Joe, Dave, and Willie went right to work on the chain. In about thirty minutes Joe's bike was ready to go again.

"Hey," said Dave, "let's climb that hill over there to check out your chain."

"Sure, let's go," answered Joe.

They all took off. Willie raced to the front. Joe and Dave went right behind him. Dust and sand were flying as they reached the top of the hill. Willie got there first. Dave was second and Joe trailed behind.

"Hi, slowpoke," Dave said to Joe. "How's the bike?"

"Not too good," said Joe. "She still slips a little."

"Can't trust those old bikes," said Willie with a grin. "You should have a good bike like mine."

"It'll be OK once I get it fixed," said Joe. "Don't worry about me."

"I don't know," Dave said. "Maybe we should call this trip off. If your bike is in trouble, maybe we should head back."

"No way, man!" Joe growled. "I came on this trip to have fun. I'm not going to head back now. My bike will be just fine. I'll fix the chain better."

"Are you sure?" Willie asked. "Maybe Dave's right. Maybe we should head back home. I sure don't want to have to carry you on my bike."

"I said it will be fine," Joe said. "Come on, let's do some riding. I'll keep up with you two."

The three riders drove their cycles around the area for about an hour. They tried small hill climbs and made some jumps. Joe put his bike through a test. He wanted to show Dave and Willie that his motorcycle was OK. Dave and Willie watched Joe ride. They knew he wouldn't quit. They knew that Joe would do his best not to spoil the trip.

Joe stopped his bike a few times and worked on the chain. After a few changes his cycle was working fine again. He made one last run up a small hill. His bike climbed the hill with ease. He waved to Willie and Dave. They waved back and went up the hill after him.

"How's it going now?" asked Willie.

"Just fine," answered Joe. "The chain is tight. It doesn't slip anymore. We don't have to give up on the trip."

Just then Dave looked over the other side of the hill. "Hey, what's that down there?" he said.

"Where?" asked Willie.

"Over there," said Dave, "to the east."

"I don't know," said Joe. "It looks like a camper van up on a jack."

"Let's take a look," said Willie. "Maybe we can help."

"Hey, what's down there?"

## Chapter 4

# Red Camper

The three riders headed down the hill. A man, woman, and a good-looking girl stood next to the camper. The riders pulled up and shut down their machines. Pulling off his helmet, Dave asked, "What's the problem? Maybe we can help."

"I don't know what the problem is. Maybe it's the fuel line or the carburetor," the man said. "It wouldn't start this morning."

"Mind if we have a look?" asked Joe. "We're pretty good with cars and motorcycles."

"Sure, help yourself," said the man. "By the way, my name is Ralph Davis. This is my wife Ann and my daughter Wendy."

All three riders said hello to Wendy. She was a pretty girl with dark hair and a friendly smile. She wore a pair of jeans and a green blouse. Joe kept looking at Wendy. Then he turned to

14

Ralph. "Let's have a look at that van."

The three riders started checking out the van. Dave checked the engine while Joe and Willie climbed underneath. Joe pulled himself out from under the truck. Then he said, "It looks like you hit a rock or something, Ralph. Your fuel line is pinched. But I think we can take it off and get the dent out of it."

"Great," said Ralph. "I've been here for three hours trying to get it started."

Joe and Willie started to take the gas line off the camper.

"Those are good-looking bikes you've got there," said Wendy. "What kind are they?"

Dave said, "Willie has a Kawasaki. Joe's is a Yamaha, and mine is a Harley Davidson."

"I have a little Honda at home," said Wendy. "But it's nothing this big."

"Want to try one out?" asked Dave.

"Sure, if you don't mind," she answered.

"Go ahead, take your pick," said Joe. "We'll be busy with the camper for awhile."

Wendy climbed aboard the Yamaha and kicked over the starter. She put it into gear. Popping the clutch, she did a short wheelie out of the camping area. Then she sped off across the sand.

"You better go with her, Dave," said Joe.

"Willie and I will fix the camper."

Dave took off after Wendy. He had to give his bike full throttle to catch up with her. They both spun some circles in the sand. Then they made some small jumps over the dunes. Wendy did pretty well on the motorcycle. She didn't seem afraid to try some tricks. Dave smiled as he watched her. She seemed like a neat girl. Maybe he could find out more about her.

Soon they came to a little spring. Fresh water in the middle of the desert was hard to find. They parked their bikes next to the spring and drank some of the water. It was cool and fresh.

"Boy, this water sure tastes good," said Dave.

"Sure does," Wendy said, wiping her chin. She took off her scarf and wet it down. Then she put it on the back of her neck.

"It feels nice and cool," she said. "Want some on your neck, too?"

"Sure," said Dave, "why not?"

Wendy wet the scarf again and put it on Dave's neck. It felt great. He liked sitting there by the spring with Wendy.

"You know," said Dave, "you're very pretty!"

"Thank you," said Wendy. She smiled at him and turned her head away.

"How long have you been on this trip with

your parents?" asked Dave.

"About two weeks," Wendy answered. "We're supposed to start back to Mill City tomorrow."

"Mill City!" said Dave. "Is that where you live? That's only about thirty minutes from where I live! I've been there lots of times. But I've never seen you there before."

"We just moved there about two months ago," Wendy said. "I'll be starting school at Mill City in a few weeks."

"Do you know anybody in Mill City?" asked Dave.

"Just a few people. Mostly kids near my house. When I start school I'll meet more people," Wendy said.

"Well, if you have any trouble meeting people, maybe I can help," Dave said.

"I'd like that," Wendy said. "I'll give you my address and phone number. Maybe we can meet sometime."

"Sure," said Dave, "That would be great!"

Dave looked at his watch. They had been gone for almost forty-five minutes. Willie and Joe had probably fixed the camper by now. It was time they started back.

"Well," Dave said, "I really like sitting here with you. But I think we better get back."

"OK, Dave." Wendy said. "I think you're right."

Dave and Wendy slipped on their helmets and pulled the visors down. The sun was bright and over 100 degrees. They kicked their bikes over with the foot starters. They dropped their bikes into first gear and took off. Sand and dust flew into the air as Dave and Wendy let out the hand clutches. They sped off across the desert once again.

## Chapter 5

# Snake Canyon

Dave and Wendy drove up to the camper. Joe and Willie were talking to Ralph and Ann.

"How is it coming?" asked Dave as he turned off his engine.

"Good as new," answered Joe. "We got the fuel line fixed and the engine running again. How did you two do?" Joe smiled at Dave and Wendy.

Dave's face turned red. "Oh, I guess we're going to really get to know each other," he said. "Wendy told me she and her folks live in Mill City."

"Great," said Willie. "Maybe we can drive over and see them sometime."

"That's what I'm hoping for," Wendy said with a smile.

Just then Ann said, "We want to thank you boys for helping us. How about staying for dinner? I can make some hot biscuits and gravy. I might even barbeque some chicken."

"Wow," Willie said. We could really go for that! Good food again!"

The three young men decided to stay for dinner. They talked to Ann and Ralph about going to Snake Canyon to test their bikes. Ralph said that he and his family would start home the next day and spend one night at Furnace Creek.

After dinner Joe, Willie, and Dave rolled out their bags near the van. Then they bedded down for the night. In the morning Anne made bacon and eggs for them with hot coffee. Then the three friends packed up their gear and got ready to leave.

"I want to thank you guys again," said Ralph. "If you hadn't come along we might still be stuck."

"No problem," said Willie. "We want to thank you for the good food. It sure beats eating beans almost every day."

They all laughed at Willie's remark. Then the boys said good-bye and started up their engines. As they rode away, Dave looked back over his shoulder. Wendy was still waving. He waved back and then threw his bike into second gear. He soon caught up with the other two riders. As he rode, Dave reached into his pocket. The paper with Wendy's address and phone number was still there.

By evening they had reached Snake Canyon. They found a small stream near the rocks and set up camp. Tomorrow they would have all day to run their bikes up the hills. Joe and Willie found some neat jumps that they could try. Dave cooked dinner that night. Franks and beans again.

## Chapter 6

# Sidewinder

The next morning they were ready to start their hill climbs. Before they took off, Dave warned his friends about rattlesnakes.

"This canyon got its name because of all the snakes around here," he said. "Be careful if you fall. There could be a snake under any of the rocks."

"You don't scare me," said Joe. "My chain is working just fine now. I'm going to ride you guys into the ground."

"Hah," said Willie. "We'll see who outrides who. Let the good times roll!"

The fire and roar of the engines echoed in the canyon. The three friends all popped their bikes into gear. Then they raced out across the rocks and sand. They shot up the small hills to test the dirt. No problem. Dave and Joe jumped a small dry creek bed. They both landed safely on the other side. Willie gunned his bike through the creek bed and up the other side. Then he slid around some rocks and drove up over a small hill. As he reached the top he gunned the engine. Then he jumped twenty feet across a small hole in the trail. He drove as though he were in a Motocross.

Dave and Joe tried to keep up with Willie. He was too fast for them though. Willie could lay his bike over until he was almost on the ground. Then he could slide around the dusty turns. Dave and Joe would always slow down and drop farther behind. There was no doubt about it, Willie could really ride.

Next they tried a steep hill. Willie went first but didn't make it to the top. His front wheel kicked out and he went flying through the air. Joe and Dave laughed. Next Dave tried. He almost reached the top but hit a rock and fell sideways into the dirt. He dusted himself off and drove back down the hill. Willie and Joe were laughing.

"All right, big shot," said Dave to Joe, "let's see you try it."

Joe slammed his bike into gear and twisted the hand throttle. He let out the hand clutch and his bike jumped towards the hill. Standing on the pedals, Joe let the bike take the shock of the bumps. Halfway up, he stepped hard on the gas and leaped up the hill to the top. He turned to see the others at the bottom of the hill. They were both clapping and cheering. Maybe Willie could run a better Motocross, but Joe could climb better.

The three friends spent all day climbing hills and speeding across the sand. Then they returned to their camp. They dusted off their cycles and checked their gas. Later on, as they ate dinner, they talked about their motorcycles. They decided that they would start back home in the morning. This would give them two days to make it if they rode hard each day. They decided that they had enough gas for the seven-hour trip to Furnace Creek. They could fill up their bikes and their spare gas cans there. Then they would head west towards home.

At seven the next morning, Dave and Willie were awakened by Joe's yelling. "Help, help! I've been bit. Help! Help! Snake bite!"

Dave and Willie jumped out of bed. They rushed to Joe. Next to Joe's bed lay a sidewinder rattlesnake. They grabbed some large rocks and threw them at the snake. One rock hit the snake right in the head. Willie picked up the snake with a long stick. Then he threw it away from the

"Help, help! I've been bit. Help! Help! Snake bite!"

camp. Joe lay on the ground groaning. Dave ran to his side.

"Take it easy, Joe. Take it easy," said Dave. He pulled out a small pocket knife., Then he yelled over to Willie. "Quick, make a small fire."

Willie didn't ask why. He collected some small sticks and some grass. In about a minute he had a fire going. Dave went to the fire and stuck his knife blade into it. The blade was soon red hot. Dave waved it in the air to cool it. He went back over to where Joe lay. He knelt down next to him. Joe's face was very white and he was breathing fast. Dave could see the sweat making bubbles on Joe's forehead.

"All right, partner," said Dave, "this is going to hurt a little. But we both know I've got to do it."

Dave bent over Joe's right leg. He could see where the snake had bitten him. The skin was red and was beginning to swell. Dave cut two deep cuts at the place where the snake had bitten Joe. The cuts began to bleed. Dave ran to his first-aid kit on his motorcycle. He took out two little rubber cups. Then he told Willie to get a blanket and a belt. Dave squeezed the cuts on Joe's leg. The blood ran freely and dripped on the ground. He squeezed the cups and put them over the bite marks. Next he took the belt and put it around Joe's leg. Then he put a stick into the belt to make a handle. He twisted the belt until it was tight. He turned to Willie.

"Get a piece of rope or something and tie this stick down," he said. "I'll cover him with the blanket. He's in shock."

Willie found the rope and fastened it to the stick. He tied it down so that it wouldn't unwind. Dave covered Joe and kept him quiet. He looked at Joe's leg. It was getting bigger and redder. He knew that he needed to get help for Joe. "OK, rest easy, Joe. We have everything under control," Dave said.

"Yeah, don't worry, man," said Willie. "Be cool."

Both Dave and Willie knew how bad a snake bite could be. They knew they had to keep Joe quiet. Dave pulled the cups off to look at the bite. It was a mess. He put the rubber cups back on. Joe groaned and tried to sit up. Dave and Willie made him lie down again.

"Rest easy, man," Willie said. "Don't try to sit up."

"Boy, I sure messed up this trip," moaned Joe. "First my bike broke, and now a snake gets me."

"Don't worry about it," Dave told him. "Just stay still. Willie and I have everything under control."

"Yeah," Willie said. "Dave took care of the bite, and we got rid of the snake."

"Fine," Joe replied, "but what are you going to do now? I can't ride my bike like this."

"You don't have to ride," Dave said. "Willie

and I will work it out."

Willie gave Joe a sip of water. Dave put some more sticks on the fire. He had to think of a plan to save Joe. He looked into the fire. How could they help Joe? Suddenly he stood up and called to Willie.

"Do you have an idea?" Willie asked.

"Yes," Dave answered. "I have a plan and I hope it works!"

## Chapter 7

# Ride for Help

Dave took Willie by the arm. He pulled him away from where Joe lay. "Look," said Dave, "we have to get help for Joe. Fast!"

"How are we going to get help way out here?" Willie asked. "We're seven hours away from a town or phone."

"I know," Dave said. "But we have to do something. We have to try. If we don't get a doctor for him he might die."

"No way! No way are we going to let him die," Willie said to Dave.

"OK" Dave said. "You get on your bike and head for Furnace Creek, Willie. I think that Joe can hold out for about six hours. If we're lucky you can make it to a phone. You can call an air rescue unit."

"Hey, man, it's seven hours to Furnace Creek. I'll never be able to make it," Willie said.

29

"Look," Dave said, "you're always saying how fast your bike is. Now you can prove it. You have to make it in less than six hours. You have to ride faster and better than ever before. You have to try!"

Willie knew that Dave was right. He knew that someone had to go for help. And someone had to stay with Joe. Dave knew first aid and he, Willie, knew how to ride fast and hard. Willie knew that it was Joe's only chance.

"OK, man," Willie said. "I can dig it. I'll do my best to make it."

Willie gathered an extra canteen from Joe's bike. Then he filled his gas tank. He filled his reserve can from Dave's extra gas. Dave was afraid and so was Willie. But they had to try. Willie kicked over his starter. His Kawasaki roared to life. This was not a time to let the good times roll. This was a matter of life and death. Willie cut his wheel towards Furnace Creek. He gunned the throttle. The Kawasaki spit fire and threw sand across the desert. He was off. The hot sun shone off his bike like a mirror. He was at full speed by the time he had gone a quarter of a mile.

Dave watched the shining bike disappear over the hill. He could still see Willie's dust for a long time. Dave turned back towards Joe. He was worried that Willie wouldn't make it in time to save Joe. But he couldn't let Joe worry, too. He had to keep him calm. Dave went over to Joe and knelt down.

"How's it going, buddy?" he asked.

"My leg hurts bad," said Joe. "Real bad."

"Don't worry," Dave said. "I cut the bite and let it bleed. I have some cups on there to suck out the poison."

"Do you think I'll be OK?" Joe asked.

"Sure," said Dave, "you'll be just fine."

Dave went down to the stream. He put some cool water on a cloth. Then he wet Joe's head to cool him off. He also rubbed some water on Joe's neck. He thought about how Wendy had put the cool scarf on his neck. He wished he had the van and the Davis family here now.

Joe was resting now. Was he still in shock? Dave didn't know. He looked at his watch. Willie had been gone for two hours now. The sun was fire hot. Would Willie be able to make it?

As it got later Dave's worry grew. He had been the one to suggest this trip. So it was his fault that Joe was hurt. If he hadn't talked the others into coming, Joe would be all right now. How could he face Joe's parents if Joe didn't make it?

How could he face Joe's other friends? He began to worry about Willie, too. What if Willie got hurt or lost in the desert? How would he be able to explain it to Willie's mom? The whole trip seemed to be a bad dream now. It was all his fault. That's all he could think of as he fell asleep in the hot sun.

# Chapter 8

# Smash Up

Willie had been riding for over two hours. The burning sun made him wet with sweat. The dust got in his mouth and made him dry. He didn't have time to stop and rest. He had to make it to Furnace Creek and get help for Joe. Willie kept his throttle wide open. The bike ran smooth and fast. He was lucky that the trail wasn't too rough. He was making good time. But could he make it in less than six hours? Willie pushed his Kawasaki to the limit. Drive, drive, drive! He *had* to make it.

Willie kept the throttle wide open. He was a good rider and a fast rider. If he didn't have any trouble, he might make it. The trail sped by under his bike. As he looked over the front wheel, he could see his shadow on the ground. He could see the outline of the bike. He could see himself leaning forward in the seat. The sun was at his back so his shadow was in front of him. Willie started to pretend he was racing. He tried to catch his shadow. He kept pushing the motorcycle faster and faster.

When he saw a rock or a hole, he leaned to one side. He sped past the rocks and ruts. His shadow stayed with him. When he moved, it moved. Willie was playing a game with himself. It helped him to keep his mind off Joe and Dave. It kept him speeding along to get help. He had to get help for Joe—and fast!

All of a sudden Willie's rear wheel locked up. The Kawasaki went into a wide skid. Willie tried to hold a line, but the bike was moving too fast. He was thrown off the motorcycle and sent tumbling against the rocks. The bike flipped over twice and landed about ten feet away. Willie was lucky because he had his helmet on. The leg of his pants was torn and he could see blood on his skin. But he could tell by the pain that it was only a scrape. "Street rash" they call it. He had scraped his legs and hands before, so he knew it wasn't bad. Willie got to his feet and knocked the dust from his clothes. His leg hurt but he could walk.

Willie looked at his motorcycle. The front wheel was badly bent. The frame was twisted.

He was thrown off the motorcycle and sent tumbling against the rocks.

The chain was broken and the sprocket was cracked. There was no way he could ride this bike, and there was no way to fix it. He thought of Joe and Dave waiting for him to bring help. What was he going to do?

"Man," thought Willie, "a fine rider you are. You can't even stay on your own bike."

Willie went over and kicked his bike. He was both mad and worried. He had to get help someway, somehow. Just then he heard the roar of a truck engine. He looked up and saw a camper van about a half-mile away. He recognized its red color. It was the Davis family! Willie climbed on top of a rock and waved his arms. He began to yell.

"Hey! Hey! Over here! Over here!" He kept yelling, "Help!, Help!"

The camper headed for Willie. They had seen him. The van stopped by the rock. Willie jumped down.

"Hi, Willie, what's up?" asked Wendy as she opened the camper door.

"It's Joe," Willie said. "He was bitten by a rattler. Dave is with him and I was supposed to go for help. I just smashed up my bike when you came along."

"Where are they?" asked Ralph.

"By the stream in Snake Canyon," answered Willie. "We have to hurry. It's been almost three hours since he was bitten!"

"We'll never make it there in time with this van," said Ralph. "Besides, I'm not a doctor and wouldn't know what to do."

"Come on, Dad. We have to do something to

help them," said Wendy.

"OK, OK, I'm thinking," said Ralph.

Just then Ann spoke up. "Why don't you use the CB radio?" she said.

"Yeah," said Willie. "Can you get an air rescue unit with that thing?"

"I don't know," said Ralph. But it's worth a try."

Ralph turned on the radio and began to tune it. There was noise and static at first. He heard a voice as he changed channels. He picked up the hand microphone and broke in.

"Breaker, breaker! This is CB Red Camper. Do you read me?"

They all waited for a moment. Then a voice came across the radio. "Hello, Red Camper, this is Sand Buggy, do you copy?"

"Yes, Sand Buggy, we copy," said Ralph. "We have a snake bite problem. Can you help?"

The radio crackled. Then the voice came on again. "Sure can, good buddy. I'm near Furnace Creek. I'll drive over there and call a doctor. What is your location? Over."

Willie took the mike from Ralph. He held it up to his mouth and spoke. "Hello, Sand Buggy. We are camped near the stream in Snake Canyon. We need a doctor or an air rescue fast. Over."

"Can do, Red Camper. I'll be on the phone in ten minutes. Over."

"Good," said Willie. "Call us back after you contact the air rescue. Over."

"Will do, Red Camper, stand by. Over."

The radio went dead. Ralph shoved the truck into gear. Then he headed for Snake Canyon.

"We'll pick up your bike on the way back," Ralph said to Willie. "Right now we can't take the time to put it on the van."

"Don't worry, man," said Willie. "Let's just get back to Dave and Joe."

They drove toward Snake Canyon. They all listened for the voice on the radio to come back on. After about fifteen minutes they heard, "Hello, Red Camper, this is Sand Buggy. Over."

"This is Red Camper," said Ralph. "Did you get the rescue team?"

"Sure did," answered the voice on the other end. "They said they know your location. They're on the way out there. Over."

"Great," said Willie. "Thanks a lot."

"No problem, Red Camper. Glad to be able to help. Over and out."

"I just hope we're not too late," said Willie softly. "I just hope."

## Chapter 9

# Rescue

Dave kept falling asleep while he was watching Joe. Each time he woke up, he checked Joe's leg. It kept getting redder and bigger. It had been almost four hours since Willie left. Dave wondered how Willie was doing. He kept hoping Willie could make it.

Dave gave Joe some more water. He wet the cloth again and wiped Joe's face. Joe was getting very hot. Dave rolled the blanket away from Joe. If it got cold, he could put it back on. Dave felt Joe's face. He could tell that Joe had a fever. How much longer could Joe hold on? Even if Willie made it to a phone, it might be too late. Again Dave thought of Joe's father and Joe's friends. If something happened to Joe, how would he ever be able to face them? Dave sat down again. He leaned against a large rock. He closed his eyes and thought about everything that was happening. The heat of the sun made him tired. In a few minutes he was asleep again.

The sound of the helicopter's engine woke up Dave. He looked over at Joe. Joe's breathing was very shallow. Dave touched him on the arm. "How you doing?" he asked.

"My leg really hurts bad," said Joe. "Is Willie back yet?"

"Not yet," Dave said. "But I hear a helicopter and I think it's looking for us. Just stay put. I'll put a wet cloth on the fire to make some smoke."

Dave wet down his towel and placed it over the fire. Thick smoke went up into the air. In just a few minutes, Dave saw the helicopter coming. It was heading straight for them. Dave stood up and began to wave his arms. "Here we are! Here we are!" he shouted. "Over here! Over here!"

The pilot saw Dave and headed for the camp. He set the chopper down about a hundred feet from where they were camping. Two men came running out from the aircraft. Dave could see their uniforms. They were from the air rescue service. "Where is the guy that's been bitten?" asked the first man.

"Right over here," said Dave.

"How long has it been since the snake bit him?" asked the second man.

Thick smoke went up into the air—Dave saw the helicopter coming.

"Almost four hours now," Dave answered. "How did you guys get here so fast?"

"Oh, we got a call from some guy on the CB radio," said the second man. "Some guy who calls himself Red Camper."

"Red Camper?" said Dave. "That means Willie must have found someone with a radio. Good old Willie. I knew he would make it."

The crew worked on Joe for about twenty minutes. The paramedic who was with the rescue team came over to Dave. He said, "Looks like you did a good job with your first aid. Your friend's going to be all right. We gave him a shot to fight the snake bite. Now we're going to fly him back to Furnace Creek to the hospital. He'll be OK in a few days."

"Thanks." said Dave. "I was really worried he might not make it."

"He'll do fine. Thanks to you and your quick thinking. Your other friend is on his way here. He's coming with the people in the camper. They should be here in about an hour."

"I'll wait for them and then come into Furnace Creek," said Dave. "Thanks again for all your help."

Dave watched as they put Joe in the chopper and took off. He felt good that Joe was going to be OK. He also felt good that Willie had made it safely. Dave started to pack up the camping gear. He wanted to be ready to leave when Willie got back.

Dave was sitting by the stream when the camper drove up. He couldn't believe it. It was Wendy and her parents' camper. The camper stopped and Willie stepped out.

"Hey," said Willie, "let the good times roll!"

Dave ran up to Willie and slapped his palms. "Boy, it's good to see you, buddy," he said. "Joe took off about an hour ago with the air rescue team. He's going to Furnace Creek."

"Come on, Dave," said Wendy. "My dad said that we can tie your bikes on the back of the camper. Then we can take you to Furnace Creek. You guys helped us. Now we get a chance to help you."

Dave helped Ralph tie the motorcycles on the back of the camper. Then they put the camping gear inside the truck. After everything was ready, they headed for Furnace Creek. On the way they picked up Willie's bike. Then they tied it on top of the camper. It was dark by the time they got to Furnace Creek.

Dave, Willie, and the Davis family went straight to the hospital. A doctor met them at the front desk. He told them that Joe was fine. Joe was asleep just then, but they could see him in the morning. Dave said that he had to make some phone calls. He would meet the others outside.

Dave called his parents and told them what had happened. Then he joined the others outside. He was looking worried.

"Hey, man," said Willie, "what's wrong?"

"Oh, I just talked to my folks. They said I probably wouldn't be going on any more trips for awhile."

"Don't worry," said Ralph. "I'll talk to your parents, all of your parents. You guys are all right. You have proven you can take care of each other. You'll probably be out here again real soon."

"I don't know," said Dave. "Staying home for awhile sounds like a good idea to me right now."

They all laughed and headed for an all-night cafe. It was time to get something to eat.

"Man," said Willie, "just wait till we get back home. I'm going to tell everybody how bad I beat you guys on my Kawasaki."

"You go right ahead and tell them," said Dave. "But don't leave out the part where you smashed it up against the rocks."

They all laughed as Willie's face got red. It felt good to have friends that you could count on when you needed them. Next year they might try the trip again.